Wellington Square

- A History -

Written and researched by

Angela Devlin and Paul Clarke

*Dedicated to all the Residents of
Wellington Square, Magazine Road, Cork,
Past, Present and Future*

With special thanks to
Marie O'Shea
for her research at the beginning of this project.

Published by
Cork Community Housing Co-op Ltd 1994 ©

Cover illustration by Paul LaRocque
Layout and design by Brendan Cotter

Acknowledgements

Our grateful thanks to:

Deirdre Ryan, Supervisor of the Wellington Square Project.

The Members of Cork Community Housing Co-op; Mr. Harold Fish, The British Council; Eamonn Young, Annmarie O' Keefe and all the staff at FÁS; Sarsfield Keating, Sless & Co; Mary Long, Facilitator; Jim Jordan and Frances Cogan, Clover Hill House; Anna Austin, Cork Civic Trust; Mary Cogan and Sean Quish, Supervalue - Centra Distribution, and to all our sponsors for their support.

Special thanks to the following who patiently assisted our research and donated photographs:

Kathleen Twomey; Con O' Connell; Gobnait O' Connell; Leslie Rice; Richard Henchion; Kieran Burke, Cork City Library; Tim Cadogan, Cork County Library; Patricia McCarthy; Captain Dan Harvey, Collins Barracks, Cork; Comdt. Peter Young; Michael Hodder, Myrtleville; D.D.C. Pochin Mould; C.J. McCarthy; Mrs. K. Leahy; Stella Cherry, Cork City Museum; John Leahy; Arthur Leahy; Boole Library, U.C.C.; Diarmuid Begley, Bandon Historical Society; Mrs. Sheila Murphy; Anna Austin, Cork Civic Trust; Dr. K.P. Ferguson, Military History Society of Ireland; Ivor Hamrock, Mayo County Library; Dr. P. McCarthy, Military History Society of Ireland; Margaret Callanan; Noelle Santry; Kevin Barber; The Staunton Family; The Barry Family; Mary Brennan; Brigader K.A. Timbers, Royal Artillery Trust, Woolwich London; Dr. J.N. Rhodes, Royal Engineers Museum, Chatham, Kent; Mr. Harold Fish, The British Council.

Sponsors

Thanks to all of the following for their support of Cork Community Housing Co-op and the Wellington Square Project:

The Department of the Environment; Cork Corporation; FÁS; Supervalue-Centra Distribution; The British Council; Bord Gais; Sless & Co.; John A. Woods; The Lough Credit Union; Telecom Eireann; The Quay Co-op; Abbey Rollers Ltd,; The Centre for Co-op Studies, U.C.C.; Beech Hill Garden Centre; Rathcooney Garden Centre; Paintwell; Southern Gas Co.; C&C; International Trading Ltd.; Douglas Court Garden Centre; Coca Cola.

Contents

Contents

Introduction

The history of Wellington Square, Magazine Rd, Cork City, in the parish of St.Finbarrs, townland of Huggartsland, parallels with some of the major happenings in two hundred years of Irish history. From the confiscation of lands in the seventeenth century and the impact of the American and French Revolutions on Irish political thought, to the United Irishmen and the Sheares Brothers of Cork. To the Militia Regiments of the 1790's whose recruits were stationed in the square to the Duke of Wellington and the battle of Waterloo of 1815 which gave the square, and No.11 their names.

From it's origins in the 18th century as a fort, a magazine, and a recruiting office for the regiments of the British Army, the square acquired it's residential character in the 1830's, with the enormous wealth of the landowners and landlords contrasting with the utter poverty of the mass of people. The stately drawing rooms and parlours of Wellington Square a world away from the Poor House on the site of the Victoria Hospital. Through wills, legacies, house deeds and marriage settlements we can see how the wealthy middle classes kept their wealth intact, at a period in Irish history when her population was reduced by 40% due to starvation and emigration, in the later half of the 19th century.

Moving through the Cork Directories of the late 19th century, we find Wellington Square retaining strong military connections with part of the square being used as a military depot, while still maintaining a thoroughly middle class character. The start of the 20th century saw the square as a prosperous residential location with houses still being rented. The Census of 1901 reveals merchants, brewers, and retired army people living there, with an upstairs, downstairs aspect to life, as some of the houses had servants. The census tells us about the changing nature of Irish life and we can observe the inhabitants through their occupations and religions, their education and languages.

The folklore of the square presents a picture of early 20th century life, with visitors being asked at the gate lodge to establish their credentials before being driven in their carriages onto the cobblestoned driveway. Memories of maids in the tunnels under the green, where presumably household stores were kept, no doubt a relic to the time of the magazine when stores of a different type were kept.

Through interviews with residents from the 1950's we have discovered a colourful history of this era. A square full of children, a meeting place for football and weightlifting clubs, containing a social mix of inhabitants in a somewhat rural setting.

The social history of Wellington Square mirrors the huge changes in Irish society over the past 200 years. Through research in Cork libraries, with contemporary material and family documents we have attempted to bring the history of the square to life. As the Housing Co-op has renovated and restored some of the buildings in the square to their previous elegance, we have attempted to recreate it's inhabitants to give a flavour of life in Wellington Square from the 18th century to the present day.

Chapter 1

18th CENTURY.
"Origins of the Magazine"

Our first documentary evidence regarding ownership of Wellington Square was found in the earliest property deed of 1770, the land being owned by Henry Sheares. On checking the " List of Sales at Chicester House" of 1701-1702 and Ordnance Survey Name Books, compiled in the 1830's we found the following:

"Humphry Sheares of Cork, apothecary, 15th March 1702, consideration, £200.17's.9d---Part of Huggartsland in the north side of Bandon Rd., in the south liberty of Corke."

Prior to this the Gould Family had owned this land in the 1640's, with Thomas Gould holding 25 acres in Huggartsland in 1688.

The Sheares family were a prosperous business family in Co.Cork who owned a considerable amount of land in the South Liberties of Cork City. Henry Sheares was a prominent banker with a town house in Nile Street (later Sheares St), a villa in Upper Glasheen, (an early Georgian House which still stands in very much it's original condition) and a country residence at Goldenbush near Bandon. A literary man and essayist who was President of the "Free Debating Society " of Cork, he established a charitable institution for the relief of people jailed for small debts. He was a Member of Parliament from 1761-1768 for Clonakilty.

A father of nine children he was to lose three sons in accidents. Robert who drowned, Richard who died in a hurricane, and Christopher who died in the West Indies of yellow fever. It is relevant and poignant to our story that his sons Henry and John Sheares were executed in 1798 for their part in the United Irishmen rebellion, at a time when Wellington Square, their father's former property, was in use as a fort and recruiting station for the regiments of the British Army, whose duty was the suppression of that movement.

Henry Sheares died in 1775 leaving his family in a wealthy position. His obituary in The Hibernian Chronicle shows the respect and esteem in which he was held.

"In public he was followed and admired, in private respected and beloved. His understanding and virtues built and ensured him an esteem and authority which no station could command, no rank could procure. He was always endeavouring to relieve the distress of the indigent, to redress the injuries of the oppressed. The charitable institutions who do honour to the City of Cork, particularly the Society for the Relief of Persons imprisoned for small debts, are principally indebted to his inventive humanity for their life, and to his activity for their continuance."

The land in Huggartsland was advertised for lease on the 7th March 1768 as follows:

"Two fields in Carrigrohane Rd.now in the possession of Captain Mercer are to be let.For any term from 1st May next. One of them contains about five acres, the other about two and three quarters. They are very near the town, in an excellent condition, walled to the road and well divided.

Inquire of Mr. Sheares, or of Mr.Michael McCarthy on Tuckeys Quay."

The property had been leased pre 1768 to Captain Richard Mercer of the Royal Irish Dragoons. He had married Ann Pigott in 1766, the daughter of Emmanuel Pigott. The latter was a Member of Parliament for Cork City and Colonel of the Regiment of Horse Militia. It is therefore quite possible that this part of Huggartsland was used for military purposes given the lessees' connections, for stabling of horses or for a stores depot of the Horse Militia.

The deed of 1770 shows that the land passed to Francis Hodder, for a nine hundred year lease with a yearly rent of £32..00. It states:

"All that and those two fields or closes situate and being next to the side of the Upper Rd leading from the said City of Cork to Carrigrohane in the South Liberties containing the whole seven acres, one rood and thirteen perches, English statute measure, be the same lately in the possession of Captain Richard Mercer, and now for sometime past in the possession of Francis Hodder."

10

At this time, what is now the Magazine Road was the main road to Carrigrohane and Macroom and remained so until the early nineteenth century when the Western Road was constructed.

...ous notice in writing under hand or Seal of such his or their intention to Surrend *...remises & all improvements now made or hereafter to be made thereon in good ten...* *And the said Francis Hodder for him his Exors Admors & Assigns doth by these* *...rant & agree to & with the sd Henry Sheares his heirs & assigns that if he the sd* *Admors or Assigns shall at any time or times hereafter break up the sd demised* *or parts thereof by plowing the same or otherwise that he the sd Francis Hodder* *Assigns shall & will lay down the same with grass seeds in good meadow Cor...* *...Years before he or they shall give notice of a Surrender Otherwise it is agr...* *...s Hodder his Exors Admors & Assigns shall not be at liberty to Surrender nor* *Sheares his heirs or Assigns be obliged to accept of such Surrender any thing* *...ise Containing to the Contrary notwithstanding And lastly the sd Henr...* *heirs & Assigns doth by these presents Covenant & promise to & with the* *...s Exors admors & Assigns that he the sd Francis Hodder his Exors admors &* *...s Respective yearly rents & performing the Covenants Clauses Conditi...* *...Contained he & they shall & may peaceably & quietly have hold possess & enjoy* *...hereby demised with the Appurtenances according to the true intent & meaning of t...* *...the term hereby granted without the let suit trouble or interruption of him the sd* *...Assigns or any person or persons lawfully claiming or to claim by from o...* *...either of them In Witness whereof the sd parties have hereunto Set their...* *...year first above Written.*

1770

Henry Sheares (seal)   Francis Hodder

COPY OF THE DEED SIGNED BY HENRY SHEARES AND FRANCIS HODDER

Francis Hodder was born in 1742, one of six children of George and Mary Hodder. His father was sheriff of Cork in 1747 and Mayor in 1754-1755.The family had their country seat in Fountainstown. Francis did not marry. He held the land until 1774 and the second deed of ownership proved to be our first clue to the military history of Wellington Square.The deed shows that the property passed to James Lill.

His death notice in the Hibernian Chronicle of 3rd October 1785 states:

"Died yesterday at the Magazine --- Lill Esq. His Majesty's Storekeeper of this City and County."

He was buried at St.Finbarrs [Cathedral] and his wife died in October 1793.

COPY OF THE DEED FROM FRANCIS HODDER TO JAMES LILL.

In 1768 the magazine for Cork City was based in Skiddy's Castle in North Main Street. This was a highly populated area of the city and there were many dangers inherent in having a magazine situated in the city centre. References in the Cork Corporation Books show that the citizens had applied for the removal of the magazine .In January 1768 the Corporation proposed that a new building for storing gunpowder should be erected in the outskirts of the city and that Skiddy's Castle should be given over to the main guard. This proposal seems to have been authorised as in 1770 the following letter was sent to the Lord Lieutenant, dated 23rd February.

"We, the Mayor and Corporation beg leave to return your Excellency our most grateful thanks for your friendship and attention to the welfare of this city of Cork, in ordering the removal of the Magazine which is in the centre of our city and which has been a constant terror to all its inhabitants, to a place of safety, and also giving up the Magazine to such public use by the Corporation as shall be approved by our worthy representative the Rt. Hon. Sergeant."

Four years later however the location of the Magazine was still causing concern. Either due to financial pressures or the slow movement of political will, it had not been moved.The Hibernian Chronicle of the 3rd January 1774 carries an article which shows the continuing fears of the citizens of Cork.

"We hear that several eminent citizens intend shortly to apply to our Representatives for the removal of that most ----- -----Skiddys Castle, where our Magazine is kept, which must ----- alarm every person possessed of the least sensibility, who cannot tell the moment the whole city may be reduced to ashes, it is ----- take fire, such melancholy catastrophes happen too frequently in other places, and surely we cannot think ourselves more secure than they. By its removal a fine passage may be opened --- -----."

A study of the Board of Ordnance Minute Books from 1773 to 1784 at the Royal Artillery Library in Woolwich, London, yielded information on the origins and building of the magazine. In the" Report of the State of Fortification, Forts,Magazines and Storehouses in Ireland" dated 1773, the following is reported regarding the city of Cork.

"That there is no fortification here but the old fort called Elizabeth Fort, which surrounds the new Barrack that can be useful. There is a stone building in the town called Skiddys Castle which is used as an Ordnance Storehouse, the inhabitants of this city having often complained of the dangerous situation of this magazine being in one of the principle streets. The powder has been removed to the Cove of Cork

which is attended with the greatest inconvenience, and should the troops of Cork be in want of powder at the time the weather is bad or blowing they could not be supplied from Cove.It is therefore proposed to build a new Magazine and Guard house on some secure spot at a proper distance from the town, so that it may be under the protection of the army, and that Skiddys Castle will remain as an ordnance storehouse only for which service there cannot be a more convenient building. The sum required for the New Magazine and Guard House will be seen in the foregoing estimate of the necessary charges of the Ordnance for two years from 31st March 1773."

James Lill leased the land in Huggartsland on the 23rd February 1774 and later that year on the 3rd May the approval of the Lord Lieutenant was given as is shown by the following entry:

"Received a letter from Secretary Blanquiere to acquaint the Board that the Lord Lieutenant approves of a new Magazine being built at Corke, but before any directions are given for proceeding thereupon that his Excellency desires they will prepare and lay before him a plan and estimate of the expense thereof, together with a description of the site, whereon they propose to erect the same.
Ordered that a Memorial with a plan and estimate be prepared accordingly."

In October 1774 James Lill, our Storekeeper received £6-16s-6d for half a years rent due to him at 30th September 1774 for the two acres of land which he had leased. One year later in September 1775, the Corporation of Cork seems to have taken the matter in their own hands. They began to measure and took a plan of a piece of land behind Elizabeth Fort with the intention of giving it to the Grand Jury. James Lill wrote to the Board regarding the situation and received the following reply:

"As by the King's instructions the Board have a right to every piece of ground belonging to the Forts and Fortifications in their kingdom.'

The actions of the Corporation seem to have produced action on behalf of the Board as the estimate for the building of the Magazine, storehouse and guardhouse was finally presented on Tuesday 6th February 1776.The Minute Book states:

"Ordered that a memorial thereupon be drawn up to his Excellency the Lord Lieutenant, representing it is absolutely necessary to have a magazine and storehouse built at Cork, the want of which is attended with great disadvantages to his Majesty's service as well as extraordinary expense, that the Board have therefore drawn up a estimate of the expense of building a Magazine and

14

Storehouse with a guardhouse amounting to £2216-11s-4d and beg leave to lay the same before his Excellency."

Work finally began on the two acres of land in Huggartsland in June 1776 when Mr.Stokes, the Clerk of Works, was ordered to repair to Cork to superintend the construction. £1050 was remitted to James Lill during the following year to pay the workmen. By April 1777 the Magazine would appear to have been completed as twelve barrells of powder were ordered to be sent to Cove. Nearly ten years had passed since Cork Corporation had made the first representations for the relocation of the Magazine from Skiddys Castle to a safer site.

The lands in Huggartsland were an excellent choice for the relocation of the Magazine to the suburbs. On the Beaufort 1801 Map of Cork the property is clearly marked as "The Fort", substantial in size, with high walls and a fortified structure located on the Macroom Rd.

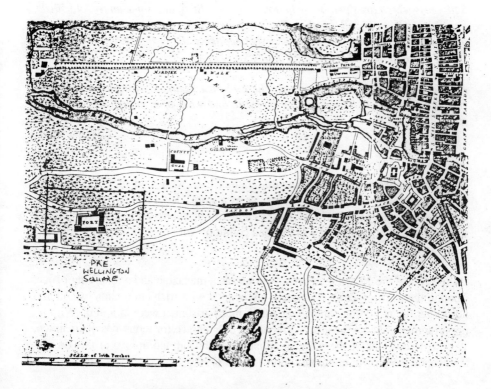

1801 BEAUFORT MAP OF CORK

15

In October 1788, Lieutenant Montgomery of the Irish Board of Ordnance visited the Fort and the following report found in the National Library sheds more light on the ownership and function of the premises at this date.

Extract from, " The Report of the Irish Board of Ordnance 1788. Report and return of Lt. Montgomery. (October 1788):

"on the 30th I arrived in Cork, and on the 31st proceeded to examine the storehouse and stores. This storehouse is built in the Fort, one mile from Cork, situated in a low wet ground, which formerly was the property of Mr. Lill, late storekeeper, and was sold by him to the Board of Ordnance, which Fort, Storekeepers house, storehouse, magazine ------- up to the Barrack Board for the use of the recruits of the English Regiments, recruiting in Ireland, for which the Artillery Barrack in the Fort was given up at the same time, and both which together with the other buildings in the Fort as I am informed by the Deputy Fort Major are since on the English Establishment.The Stores are lodged in the Sallyports which are open at the bottom, next the ditch, and some under old sheds, but exposed to rain and weather. The carriages of the guns very much scaled and abused by the recruits, and the round shot scattered about the Fort. The magazine stands much in need of a door lock and key.

The Fort seems very much neglected. The Embrasures and Merlons being almost in ruin, and the gracis by the turning of cattle and want of attention, in a very bad state."

October 1788.

We can surmise from this report that James Lill, who died in 1785, sold the property to the Board of Ordnance for use as a stores depot and magazine,and that later it was used by the Barrack Board as a recruiting centre for English Regiments. It would appear that the Fort was in a bad condition with no door lock or key on the magazine.

By the end of the 1780's the Fort was in use as a magazine and a recruiting office. Though the town of Cobh is normally associated with Irish emigration, we should not forget the recruiting stations, in which many Irishmen were to join up.With no opportunities at home the army offered the only choice for thousands of Irishmen. We must now look at the political situation in Ireland and abroad at this time to understand the growth in military forces in the 1790's.

The undercurrent caused by the French Revolution in 1789 had begun to influence

Irish political thought. The society of the United Irishmen was formed in 1791 for the reform of the Dublin parliament and the emancipation of Catholics. The society issued the following manifesto:

"The object of this Institution is to make an United Society of the Irish nation, to make all Irishmen Citizens -- as distinct from subjects -- all Citizens Irishmen. Peace in this island has hitherto been a peace on the principles and with the consequences of civil war. For a century past (since the Boyne) there has indeed been tranquility but to most of our dear country men it has been the tranquility of a dungeon, and if the land has lately prospered, it has been owing to the goodness of providence and the strong efforts of human nature resisting and overcoming the malignant influence of a miserable administration."

Agitation for Catholic emancipation continued until 1793 when the Catholic Relief Act was passed.But it ceded only partial relief. Those with property qualifications could sit on borough corporations and county juries. Higher qualifications were needed for the vote in parliamentary elections but Catholics could not stand as candidates.In 1793 France declared war on England, and the United Irishmen who openly supported the ideals of the French Republic were suppressed. When they re-established in the following year, they did so as a secret organization enlisting help from the French Directory.

"Erin Go Bray" - a loyalist view of the "Allied Republics of France and Ireland".

The cartoon above of "Erin Go Bray", by Samson, published in London in 1798 shows the anti republican feelings towards the "Allied Republics of France and Ireland." The symbols of Church and Monarchy being crushed underfoot by the rider and his donkey, under the auspices of the devil who is viewing the scene from the sidelines.

The French expedition to Ireland in 1796, with the attempted landing at Bantry Bay of 15,000 French troops, was hampered by severe weather which eventually led to its failure. The crown forces in Co. Cork at this time were inadequate to cope with the threatened invasion. Figures given for the British military forces in Co. Cork were 3,000, but by 1797 the military force in Ireland had risen to nearly 77,000 men, incorporating the regular soldiers, the Militia, and the Yeomanry, the latter being embodied in 1796.

Of interest to Wellington Square are the movements of the Militia. When No.11 was being renovated two pieces of graffiti were found on one of the inside walls underlaying old plaster. The first had the date 1791 but the lettering around it was illegible. However the second piece of graffiti bore the inscription "North Mayo Militia Reg," with a date of 1797.

Movements of the Militia were extremely difficult to trace, as they were posted throughout Ireland, but research into this regiment proved rewarding in relation to No.11.The North Mayo Militia were formed in 1793 with their headquarters in Ballina, under the command of the Rt. Hon. James Cuffe, Barrack Master General of Ireland. Terry Reilly in his article,"Dear Old Ballina," mentions that Ballina remained the headquarters of the regiment though the soldiers were stationed around the country.

They were sent to Cork in 1797 as part of the forces to resist the French landing at Bantry Bay. The Light Company were transferred to Co.Wexford and fought at Gorey, Vinegar Hill and Wexford town. Six companies of the regiment remained stationed at Cork.

Another mention of the North Mayo Militia occurs in the " Council Book of the Corporation of Cork" of the 2nd April 1798, which would prove their connection with Cork. It states:

" That Major General Myers, Commander the Garrison of Corke be presented with his freedom in a silver box with a suitable acknowledgement of the sense this Board entertains of the good conduct of him and the garrison under his command, also that Lieut. Col. John Finlay Com the Dublin Militia now part of this garrison, William Wilson Esq. Major of the 2nd Fencible Regiment of Light Dragoons, Maurice Blake Esq. Major and now commanding the North Mayo Regiment, George Kay Esq. Major and now commanding the Elgin Fencibles Regiment, be presented with their freedom".

18

The North Mayo Militia returned to Ballina in May 1802. They fought in the Napoleonic and Crimean Wars. In 1881 they were affiliated with regular regiments of the Irish Infantry, the North Mayo becoming the 6th Battalion Connaught Rangers.The finding of the graffiti in No.11 with the date of 1797 would suggest that the Fort was a temporary barracks during the 1790's.

1798 The United Irishmen and the Sheares Brothers.

The failed rebellion in 1798 of the United Irishmen saw the executions of John and Henry Sheares, whose father Henry had owned the land in Huggartsland thirty years previously. It is poignant that Wellington Square was at this time in use as a recruiting station and Fort for the members of the British regiments, and that the Militia who played a large part in the suppression of the United Irishmen had a connection to it.The following extract from a poem by J. Fraser expresses the feelings towards the army regiments.

" Edward Molloy"
1798
" A Reminiscence of Troubled Times"

"What use in delaying for vengeance to strike?
Has each bosom a heart ? has each shoulder a pike?
On,On, to Rathangan, 'tis full to the gorge,
With the red handed ruffians of black hearted George;
Who stabbed with their bayonets, in search of pike heads,
The thatch of our cabins, and ticks of our beds;
Who lashed us like hounds, till we reddened our tracks
From triangle to threshold, with blood from our backs;
The cruel destroyer 'tis just to destroy --
What says our young captain, brave Edward Molloy ?"

The Sheares brothers were born at Goldenbush, Co. Cork and spent their childhood in Glasheen. They were educated at Trinity College, both studying law, and after being called to the bar they resided permanently in Dublin. They visited France in 1792 and influenced by the French Revolution and its republican ideals they joined the United Irishmen in 1793. The organization being intent on parliamentary reform at that time. Neither of the brothers came to prominence in the society until March 1798, when most of the members of the Leinster Directory were arrested.

John Sheares became a member of the Leinster Executive. He was to travel to Cork in June to assist in the movement there but was arrested with his brother on the 21st June 1798. They were betrayed by a member of a militia regiment, Captain Armstrong. The following extract from a handwritten manifesto by John Sheares, found in his house in Baggot St, Dublin, was used extensively by the Commission for High Treason to prove the case against them.It begins:

" Irishmen -- your country is free -- That vile government which has so long and so cruelly oppressed you -- is no more."

After being tried on the 12th and 13th July both prisoners were found guilty. Though both brothers insisted that they were not involved in insurrection and solely interested in parliamentary reform, they were hanged on the 14th July 1798. They were interred in St. Michan's churchyard in the north side of Dublin.

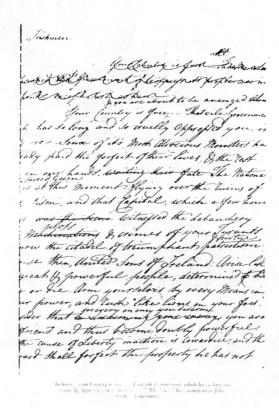

THE REPORT OF THE SECRET COMMITTEE OF THE HOUSE OF COMMONS, DUBLIN, 1798

Chapter 2

19TH CENTURY.
"A Residential Square"

The failed rising in 1798 led to the ending of Grattan's Parliament and in 1800 to the Act of Union with Great Britain. Events on the continent with the Napoleonic wars continuing would eventually lead to the Battle of Waterloo in 1815. The City of Cork at this time was extremely important to British naval interests. Threats of invasion from the French led to the fortification of Cork harbour. The port of Cork had established a victuling and provision trade for the navy. From the late 18th century to 1815 Britain was at war with France and the City of Cork played an important part in providing supplies for the army and navy.

In 1801 construction began on Collins Barracks which saw it's completion in 1806. It was originally known as the Royal Barracks and housed 156 officers and 1994 men. The continuous threat of invasion from the French would appear to have preoccupied the military establishment, as the Martello Towers built in Cork Harbour can be dated to 1813-1815, much later than their Dublin counterparts which were constructed in 1804. The gunpowder mills at Ballincollig were opened in 1794 by Charles Leslie and John Travers. They were later sold to the Board of Ordnance in 1805 during the Napoleonic wars.

It would appear that Wellington Square was not classed as a "Fort"by 1803. A letter from Dr. John Rhodes, Curator of the Royal Engineers Museum in Kent of 16th November 1994 states:

"A map of 1803 drawn up by a Col Twiss RE shows the forts and their ordnance guarding the approaches to the city including Charles Fort, Kinsale and Oysterhaven Fort as well as those commanding Cork Harbour. On the possible site of your 'fort' SW of the city there is a configuration on the map which could represent a former defensive structure, but it is not listed or highlighted by Col Twiss as a fort still in use in 1803."

By 1803 the construction of Collins Barracks was well under way and presumably the structure at Wellington Square was falling into decline and not being repaired as necessary. As the Ordnance Board had bought Ballincollig Gunpowder Mills in 1805 there was no continuing need for a magazine in Huggartsland.

ARTHUR WELLESLEY
DUKE OF WELLINGTON

It is from this period that Wellington Square acquired it's name. On the 1801 Beaufort Map of Cork it is referred to as " The Fort ", but on gaining it's residential nature in 1832 it was called after the Duke of Wellington . The folklore of the square has always held that Arthur Wellesley, the Duke of Wellington had some connections with the Fort. Though this cannot be proved, Wellington had his officers' quarters near Barrack St. which is situated one mile from the square. In 1787 he was a lieutenant in the 58th regiment and carried the colour in the guard when the future King William IV visited Cork. As Wellington Square was used as a recruiting station it is highly probable that he did have an association with it.

In 1807 Wellesley toured Ireland, from Dublin to Cork, inspecting Martello towers, barracks and other military establishments, making recommendations for improvement. After the Battle of Waterloo in 1815,when Napoleon was defeated, it was fashionable to name streets and buildings after the famous victory and persons connected with it. For example, we find in Cork, Waterloo Terrace, Wellington Road, and Wellesley Terrace. The large house in the square, No.11, being known as Waterloo House.

Moving into the 1820's an inspection of the Tithe Applotment Books of St. Finbarrs Parish of 1828 shows the property being mentioned as "The Magazine Land". This was our last reference to the official military history of Wellington Square as four years later in 1832 we find the property had changed hands.The name on the Applotment Books for 1832, as the land occupier was Henry Osburne Seward.

1830's

The start of the 1830's would see the premises change from it's military role to a residential location but still retain army connections. From being called the "Magazine Land " on St. Finbarrs Tithe of 1828, we find the name of Wellington Square appearing on maps of the 1830's. The pillars at the entrance of the square bear the date of 1832. It was around this time that Henry Osburne Seward acquired possession of the lease . He built the other houses in the square adjoining and facing No.11. As the suburbs around Cork city were becoming popular places to live we find the following advertisement in The Constitution of 21st August 1832. We should take note of it's previous name "Late Magazine".

"WELLINGTON SQUARE (LATE MAGAZINE)"

" To Let, several houses just finished, of different sizes, with gardens to each, with or without coach house or stables. The rent will be moderate ---not subject to city taxation, and not requiring any outlay, being finished in the best manner, with every accommodation for the immediate reception of respectable families.

Some of the houses have 3 sitting rooms, 4 to 6 bedrooms, dressing room, closets, pantries,and large basement stories etc.Others have 2 sitting rooms, 4 to 5 bedrooms etc; and a neat cottage, 2 sitting and 3 bedrooms etc. Good kitchens to each, fitted up with a hot hearth, grate, oven etc. and well enclosed yards.

There is an abundance of the finest spring water on the premises, the air is good, the soil dry, and the situation extremely healthy and convenient ; it commands a view of the most beautiful part of Sunday's Well and the surrounding country, is within a few minutes walk of the Bishop's Palace and about 400 yards of the new Western Road, by a good carriage road recently put in order,which runs in front of the new entrance to the square. Persons taking a lease will have a preference, a term of 800 years can be given, and the rent may be fined down if required.

Apply personally, or by letter, on the premises to Mr. Henry Osburne Seward; or at his house Sidney Place.

The centre of the square will be a green, with a carriage drive round the terraces, and inside the gate on each side will be immediately planted with shrubs etc.
A large quantity of very good pavement stones for sale."

To be exempt from city taxation --the square being situated outside the municipal boundary, to have an abundant supply of fresh water, and to have the security of high walls would have made Wellington Square an ideal place to live. With the added advantage of a carriage road--as Cork had no public transport until the 1850's--and the city centre within 20 minutes walk the location was suited to those with business in town. As the wealthier citizens of Cork city had begun their move to the suburbs, carriages were extremely important, and many newspaper advertisements would mention coach houses or stables as being available.

The advertisement expresses the ideals of the middle classes in looking for residences for respectable families. They had the security of high walls and an entrance gate with a porter's lodge, away from the poverty and violence of the inner city. "An abundance of the finest spring water", good air and a healthy situation offered protection from the outbreaks of disease common in the overcrowding of the city. Houses were large enough to accommodate servants, nannies and housekeepers with pantries and basements.Another interesting aspect to the square is noted in the following advert which appeared in The Southern Reporter and Cork Commercial Courier, one year later on Saturday evening 23rd February 1833.

"TO BE LET
AT WELLINGTON SQUARE (LATE MAGAZINE)"

" Some very neat and well finished houses and cottages, different in sizes with every convenience for respectable families, gardens to each ---- coach house and stables if required --- not subject to city taxes ---- an abundant supply of best spring water on the premises. A very neat entrance gate of cut stone, inside which is a porter's lodge; the ground is well enclosed.

The centre of the square is a large green, planted with shrubs enclosed with iron railing, round which there is a carriage drive. The whole of the ground is neatly laid out with shrubberies, walks, terraces and garden, planted with evergreens, forest trees, flowering shrubs and creepers. It commands a view of the most beautiful River Lee, Sunday's Well, Wilton, Lehena and the surrounding scenery. The situation is particularly well suited for families. The walls are sufficiently extensive, the air is good. The soil dry and healthy on a rising bed of limestone. A carriage road runs in front of the entrance to the new Western Road which is within about 500 yards, 10 minutes walk from the Bishop's Palace, and 20 minutes to the parade.

Application to be made to Henry Osburne Seward Esq.,
Sidney Place either personally or by letter.   *Feb 12th."*

Whereas the green in the centre of the square was not laid out in 1832, the 1833 advertisement gives great emphasis to the description of the newly laid out gardens, with shrubberies, walks, evergreens and creepers. The rural atmosphere evoking a sense of peace and tranquillity which the wealthy middle classes desired, contrasting with the social disadvantages of urban dwelling. As the gardens and green were given such importance in 1833, it is worthy to note that the Housing Co-op has restored part of those gardens, and that a Resident's Committee has been set up to restore the green. As the houses have been renovated, so to have the gardens with as much planning and detailed attention to shrubs, walks and greenery as occurred in 1833. The following map of Cork in 1841 shows Wellington Square in close proximity to two nurseries where perhaps the first gardening supplies were bought.

SEE MAP OVERLEAF

Though the adverts suggest that Wellington Square was a healthy place to live, with good air and fresh springwater, the following death notice, 14 years later in the Southern Reporter, Tuesday 14th August 1847 states,

"on the 12th inst. at his father's residence, Wellington Square, of cholera, Julius youngest son of John Besnard Jnr. Esq."

The Besnard Family were sailmakers in the 18th century, and they were involved in the brokerage trade for merchants and masters of ships. It would appear that Wellington Square was not immune to disease.

Henry Osburne Seward

Pigots directory of 1824 names Henry Osburne Seward as of noble gentry, living in Sidney Place, Cork City. He later moved to Lee Cottage beside the Old County Gaol. Originally from Newcastle West, Co. Limerick, the family owned land in Huggartsland, Douglas, Youghal, Fermoy and Co. Limerick.

Seward owned a large part of Douglas Village, including being landlord of the RIC Barracks and Courthouse, St. Columbas' Church, The Dispensary and National Schoolhouse. He applied for a coat of arms in 1844 to the Chief Herald - and this application tells us of his family history - from Devonshire originally and

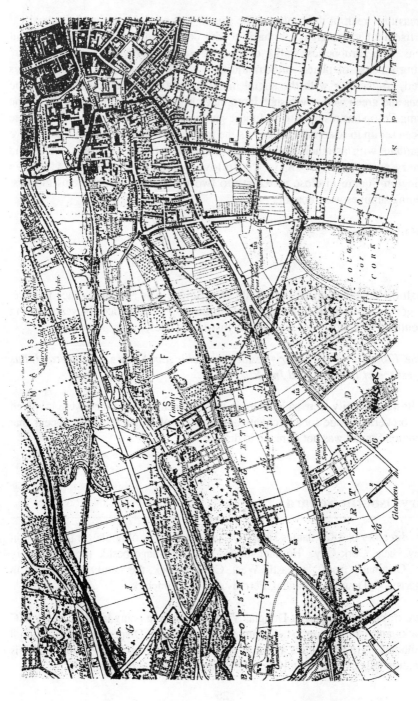

1841 MAP OF CORK SHOWING WELLINGTON SQUARE IN THE VICINITY OF TWO NURSERIES

intermarriage with the Osburne family of Ayrshire and Mid Lothian in Scotland. The Chief Herald's reply is as follows:

"To all and singular to whom these presents shall come, I, Sir William Bethan, Knight attendant on the most Illustrious Order of Saint Patrick, Ulster, King of Arms, and Principal Herald of all Ireland, send Greeting. Whereas application has been made to me by Henry Osburne Seward of Lee Cottage and Douglas, in the county of Cork, and descended of an ancient Family, originally of Devonshire from where his immediate ancestors passed over to Ireland, and settled in the counties of Waterford and Cork, That, his Family having long used armorial bearings, and being by his father's intermarriage with the ancient Family of Osburne, of Ayrshire and Mid Lothian in Scotland, entitled to certain quarterings of arms, he is now desirous that all such should be duly marshalled and confirmed by lawful authority and has therefore prayed that I would grant and confirm to his and his descendants, such arms as he and they may lawfully use and bear."

His application was successful as confirmation of arms was granted in July 1844.

Though all the above would suggest Osburne Seward as a member of the Cork gentry, his father Charles was a victualler at 165, Blarney Street, where he lived until his death, his son Henry who was born in 1793 and died in November 1854, would appear to have held greater social ambitions and began to buy land after his father's death. Henry had six daughters and two sons. One of his sons died in infancy of croup in 1827 - but his son Henry Jnr. attended Trinity College Dublin. Henry Jnr. died in 1849, aged 26, no doubt a terrible blow to his father and family.

Some of Henry Osburne Seward's family papers are kept in the Boole Library, UCC, and we found marriage settlements, legacies and a copy of his will. These papers are pretty extensive and his will gives us an insight into how the wealthy middle classes conducted their affairs, and how their wealth was kept intact.

His will was dated December 1842 and renamed unchanged at his death in 1854. It contains information regarding the rights of women in the 19th century. It states:

"and Testator further Bequeathed unto his said wife Anne Seward all his Household furniture, Plate, Linen, China, Wines, Spirits, Utensils and carriages - and further that his said wife should be at Liberty to continue to reside at his then residence Lee Cottage - paying a yearly rent of £60 therefore to commence six months after his decease to his personal Estate."

The campaigns in the 19th Century aimed at improving the situation of women, eg. in political and educational spheres, etc. also included a demand for married womens property rights. When a woman married her property was claimed by her husband and it was not until the Married Womens' Property Acts of 1870, 1874 and 1882 that married women were allowed to own property. Wives and daughters of the wealthy middle classes were totally dependant on their husbands and fathers and not expected to follow careers. So we find Mrs. Seward paying £60 per annum to her deceased husbands estate.

"The said rent to form a portion of his assets"

She was however not left a pauper. She would receive £400 annually from rents due from their lands, in Douglas.

The will also directs:

"his said Trustees to pay unto each and every of his daughters, Mary, Matilda, Henrietta and Lucy, the sum of £4,000 a piece, payable at their respective ages of 25 years, or on days of their marriage, whichever should first happen, provided such marriage be with the Consent of any two of his trustees, for the time being one of whom to be his wife."

The Misses Seward had no freedom in choosing prospective husbands.

In the case of Mrs. Seward, no longer wishing to reside in Lee Cottage:

"the Testator directed his said Trustees to let sell or dispose of said residence, reserving the passage leading to Wellington Square."

This presumably was a private passage way and given the expanding nature of the western suburbs of Cork City could be a valuable asset, for at this time carriages were extensively used for transport.

We also find reference to another daughter, Anne Elizabeth Seward, now the wife of the Reverend William Worth Hoare, living in Staley Bridge, England. She was bequeathed £150 by her father but would only receive it on the condition, *"as soon as she should come to reside in Ireland but not before.".*

She was also left an annuity of £50, with the above condition attached. Whether Anne Elizabeth married or moved to England without her father's permission is not known, but would certainly seem to have caused her father concern.

Henry Osburne Seward left an annuity of £50, also from the rents of Douglas to his sister Sarah Greenham for her sole benefit, as the following words make clear:

"for her separate use exclusively of her present or any after taken husband."

Most of Osburne Seward's Assets were left originally to his son Henry Jnr. who had died in 1849. The Cork Constitution of the 6th of January 1849 reports:

"Died on the 3rd Inst., at Ventor, Isle of Wight, Henry Osburne Seward Esquire Junior, aged twenty six years, only son of H. Osburne Seward Esquire, Lee Cottage, Cork."

When Henry Osburne Seward died in 1854 at his son-in-law's residence at Woodlands, Cheshire, his assets passed to his surviving daughters Mary, Lucy, Matilda, Henrietta and Anne. They would eventually pass to Henrietta's two sons, Charles and Henry. Henrietta had married Charles Cheetham Bayley of Chester on 15th February 1846, and was paid the sum of £3,000 as part of her fortune of the £4,000 legacy. In 1855, the Bayleys bought out their share of the family fortune for £6,875, leaving Wellington Square and other properties to Mary, Matilda and Lucy, the unmarried sisters, who continued to live at Lee Cottage, with their mother.

There is an interesting handwritten note at the end of the document on which the Bayleys had bought out their share of the family fortune. Written by one of the solicitors, it tells of how Henrietta was taken to a separate room and asked if she fully understood the contents of the documents and what it would entail if she signed. She replied yes. As this was before the Married Women's Property Acts, it was her husbands name on the document to which she signed.

Henry Osburne Seward's will gives us an insight into the enormous wealth of the gentry as compared with the majority of citizens in Cork. Having left £4,000 a piece to four of his daughters, it is worth noting some of the average daily wages in Cork in the 1850's. Boilermakers-5 shillings, Cabinet makers-5 shillings, weavers - 1 shilling to 3 shillings, general labourers-1 shilling 4d to two shillings. In the days of no social welfare the contrast is striking.

It would appear from the Household Accounts of the Misses Seward who inherited Wellington Square in 1854, that the houses in the square were kept in good order with sewers being cleared and houses being repaired, for example: Mr. J. Regan was paid £24-9s-6d for his work in repairing four of the houses in 1866. The clearing of the sewers cost 3s and 6d, with a further £1-00-0d for another house repair. We also find that £1-4s-6d was paid for work on the pump.

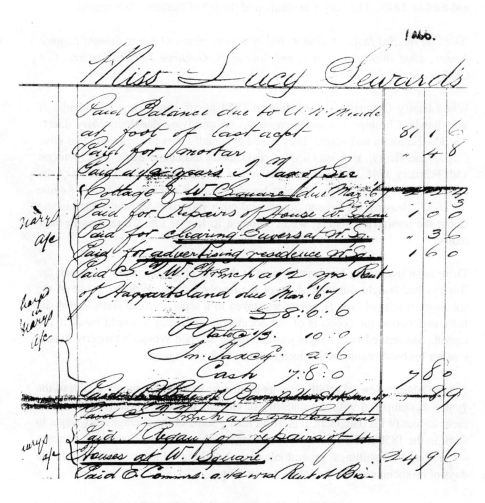

MISS LUCY SEWARDS ACCOUNTS 1866.

Mary, Lucy and Matilda Osburne Seward died within the one year, Mary in November 1866, Lucy in July 1867 and Matilda in September 1867. Their mother survived them and died in 1877, aged 89 years. Matilda's will suggests that the three sisters were involved in charitable societies as were many Victorian ladies.

Their mother Mrs. Anne Seward was a patroness of the Cork Industrial School, whose objective was to *"afford occupation to young females, of good character, so as to enable them to obtain a livelihood. It was established chiefly for girls at that period of life which intervenes between their leaving the Parochial School and entering service, or otherwise engaging in business - a period at which they are especially exposed to temptation."* The Constitution 25.11.1854 (Advert for a sale of work with the band of the 91st regiment attending at the Imperial Clarence Rooms.)

Matilda's will states:

" I give devise and bequeath the rents of Droumleigh, Gurtcronatry, Carrycrohane and Gurtnacarrigy and Coolnacranage situated in the Barony of West Muskerry, to be annually applicable to the purposes of the following charities, The Society for Conversion of the Jews -- The Church Missionary Society and the Cork Protestant Orphan Society."

A £20 annuity was left to her cousins Emily and Hetty Seward who resided at Wellington Square.

Henry Osburne Bayley (her nephew) of Ardwick, Manchester, was named as sole executor to administer her just debts and legacies contained in her will.

"I leave devise and bequeath to my said nephew Charles Bayley, Wellington Square and the lands of Gurteenaspig and Huggartsland adjoining Wellington Square in the County of Cork, and also the dwelling house and lands of Lee Cottage after the death of my said dear mother."

Her niece Henrietta Bayley received *"the land of Ballyvoluge in the county of Cork and the house and premises at Sidney Place."*

Wellington Square passed to Charles Scot Bayley in 1867, the grandson of Henry Osburne Seward, whose daughter Henrietta had bought out her share is his assets for £6875.

The Seward family are buried in St. Lukes graveyard in Douglas. The Coat of Arms with the three crests can still be seen. The family motto of "once we were" chillingly predicting the death of Henry Osburne Seward and his two sons who died before him.

THE OSBURNE SEWARD COAT OF ARMS IN ST. LUKES GRAVEYARD, DOUGLAS.

Life In The Square

The Cork directories of the 19th century have been invaluable in trying to recreate the social life in the square, who lived there and what employment did they pursue?. Was there still a military influence involved? What was the social position of the inhabitants? Though the general valuation of rateable property or Griffith's valuation of 1852 does not list occupations we can surmise from it that there were twelve houses in the square at this time.

We find Henry Osburne Seward as the immediate lessor of Wellington Square. This valuation of 1852, shows land and house occupiers, acreage and the total annual valuation of rateable property. The valuation was based on rent potential. It is also an interesting guide to the structure of sub letting in property matters. Though the rural valuations are more helpful than the urban, we can surmise that Wellington Square was an elite and pretty expensive place to rent (see opposite).

Huggart's land 1852 (Ord. S. 74) OCCUPIERS	IMMEDIATE LESSORS or LANDLORDS.		AREA A. R. P.
Edward M. Fitzgerald	Alicia Berry Sheers	House offices & land	1 . 3 . 38
Richard Toban	Edward M. Fitzgerald	House	
Samuel Pleazby	Alicia Berry Sheers	House offices & land	3 . 2 . 9
Samuel Pleazby	Bart William Smith	Land	2 . 2 . 33
Mary Lynch	Alicia Berry Sheers	Land	3 . 0 . 27
Maurice Rue se	Mary Lynch	House	—
Edward Russell	Same	House	—
Mary Lynch	Robert Honner	House offices & land	0 . 3 . 28
Johanna Murphy	Mary Lynch	House	—
Thomas Carroll	John Green	House offices & garden	0 . 0 . 10
Jeremiah Pouney	Mary Lynch	House offices & garden	0 . 0 . 10
Edward Sullivan	Same	House offices & garden	0 . 0 . 10
Daniel Lenaghan	Same	House offices & garden	0 . 0 . 10
Jeremiah Bryan	Same	House offices & garden	0 . 0 . 10
John Lenihan	Same	House office & garden	0 . 0 . 10
		Land under Houses	0 . 0 . 31
Michael Gainey	Alicia P. Sheers	Land	7 . 0 . 0
Cornelius Kiely	Michael Gainey	House	—
Denis Horrigan	Same	House	—
Samuel Pleazby	Henry O Seward	Land	4 . 2 . 28
Patrick McCarthy	Samuel Pleazby	House	—
Samuel Pleazby	Henry O Seward	Land	2 . 3 . 28
Patrick Keane	Samuel Pleazby	House	—
Henry O Seward	Alicia P. Sheers	Land	1 . 0 . 21
James Galvin	Henry O Seward	House (gate lodge	
Arthur C. Henley	Same	House & sm garden	
Unoccupied	Same	House & sm garden	
William Woods	Same	House & sm garden	
William Hincks	Same	House & sm garden	
Alex Kingston Fox	Same	House & sm garden	
William G. Jones	Same	House & sm garden	
Belinda Seward	Same	House & sm garden	
Jane & E. Eason	Same	House & sm garden	
John Blyth	Same	House offices & garden	0 . 1 . 0
Henry O Seward	Alicia P. Sheers	Offices	—
Alex Kingston Fox	Henry O Seward	Offices	—
Charles R. Dickenson	Same	House	—
Unoccupied	Same	House	—
		Waste of Lot	0 . 3 . 30

GRIFFITH'S VALUATION 1852

From James Galvin living in the gate lodge at £2-10-0 (annual rateable valuable) to the Misses Seward, nieces of the landlord at £10-10-0, to John Blyth who rented "House, offices and garden" at £32-0-0. It shows that twelve houses were in the Square at this time as borne out by the street directories of the 1860's. In the following advertisement of the Cork Examiner of Monday 28th July 1856, we find reference to Number 11 being called "Waterloo House" a large and commodious house, and to other houses being offered for rent - still free of city taxation.

CHEAP AND DESIRABLE RESIDENCES, FREE OF CITY TAXATION.

TO BE LET, a few moderate-sized convenient Houses, at WELLINGTON SQUARE, fit for Respectable Families; also the Large and Commodious House in the same Square, known as Waterloo House. These Houses have been lately painted and put in perfect order.

The Lodge-keeper at Wellington Square will show the houses.

Apply on Saturdays to ADAM N. MEADE, Office, 15, Morrison's Quay, Cork; or by Letter on other days, directed to River View, Enniskeane, Bandon. (487)

The 19th Century History of Wellington Square as remembered by the older residents from the 1920's, has always given emphasis to the military associations of it's occupiers. For example, retired army people and their families. Robert H. Laings, Cork Mercantile Directory of 1863 gave us further proof that this was so, with a direct military reference. It lists the residents as follows:

WELLINGTON SQUARE 1863

1. Stevenson, Captain Andrew.

2. Duncan Robert ,Co-inspector.

4. Seward, the misses.

6. McCarthy, Charles (McC and Co.).

8. Bennet, Mrs. Jane.

10. Allen, Peter.

11. Smith, Matthias.

12. Daly, Jas (Quarter Master Sergeant).

and also a note as follows:
Permanent Staff of the Militia.

"5th or Royal Cork City Artillery - (Depot Wellington Square) Col. The Earl of Bandon; Lieut-Col Andrew Jordan Wood; Adjutant, Captain A. Stevenson. Agents, Cane and Sons, Dublin Facings Red."

It would appear that as late as 1863, part of Wellington Square was still in use as a depot for the Royal Cork City Artillery with their Adjutant Captain A. Stevenson living in No. 1 and their Quarter Master Sergeant Jas Daly inhabiting No. 12. The folklore of the square remembers stables attached to No. 12 with children from the 1940's playing with horse shoes that had been found. As we move four years later to 1867, Henry and Coghlans Munster Directory seems to show that the military connection was disappearing. This directory lists the occupation of the male occupiers but not the female. It shows:

WELLINGTON SQUARE 1867.

1. Bickford. Robert John, Clerk.
   Barter. Ann Mrs.
2. Warren. C.D. Captain.
3. Vacant.
4. Seward. Misses the.
5. Vacant.
6. McCarthy Charles Draper.
7. Smith. Matthias gentleman.
8. Bennet. Jane Mrs.
9. Vacant.
10. Allen, Peter. Draper's assistant.
11. Vacant.
12. Bergin. Michael, clerk.

No. 1 and No. 12 would appear to have ceased their connection to the Royal Cork City Artillery. However, No.2 was inhabited by a Captain C.D. Warren. There is still a distinctly middle class ethos to the square. This is emphasised further in Guys Directory of 1875 (Page 594) which lists the inhabitants and their occupation as follows.

35

WELLINGTON SQUARE 1875

Carpenter.	John
Carr	Robert
Clery	Richard E. Sec. Chamber Commerce
Compton	Charles
Daly	William, House and Land Agent
Hare	Jonathan George, Clerk.
Johnston	Edward Ruby. Timber merchants.

The female heads of Households are not named as presumably they had no business interests. The occupations of the residents suggest a commercial background to the social standing of the square. There is no mention of military associations at this time.

We know that No. 4 was still inhabited in 1874 by Emily Seward, a niece of Henry Osburne Seward as in a letter (shown opposite)to her cousins the Greggs - she tells of the death of her sister Hetty on September 13th (letter dated 14th February, 1874, headed No 4 Wellington Square).

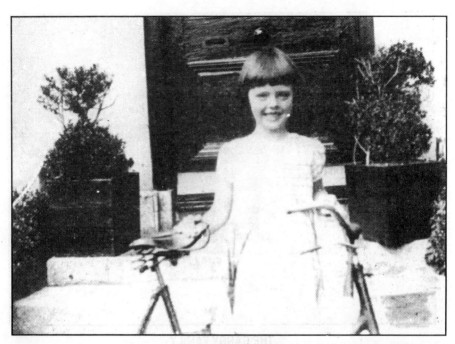

THE BARRY FAMILY

THE BARRY FAMILY

June 1946 - **Bill, John** and **Mary Leahy**

1929

Peg O'Leary (right) sister-in-law of Mrs. McSweeney, originally from Farnanes, Co. Cork, home on holidays from Philadelphia, seen here with Mrs. McSweeney's sisters

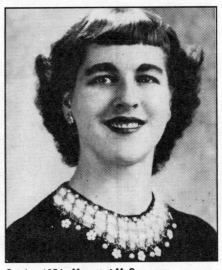

1963 - Catherine McSweeney of No.5 Wellington Square.

October 1954 - Margaret McSweeney, daughter of Catherine McSweeney.

Bernadette, Kathleen, Louise and **Mary Leahy**

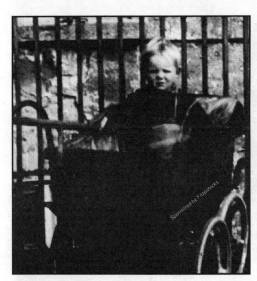

1948 - **Artie Leahy!**

1994 - Claire, Anne **and** Philomena Staunton

Circa 1946 - **Andrew Leggett**

Billy Leahy

The Leggett family

1. **Andrew Leggett,** circa 1946
2. **Billy Leahy**
3. **The Leggett family**
4. **Arthur Leahy** with **Billy** and **Artie**
5. **Kathleen Leahy**
6. **Catherine** and **Andrew Leggett**
7. **Mrs. Hennessy** with **Arthur Leahy**

June 1946 - Breda O'Connell

Mary Aherne and Bertie Barry

Dan McSweeney and friends outside No.11

Chapter 3

20th CENTURY
"Life in the Square"

A t the beginning of the 20th Century, Wellington Square was owned by Charles Scot Bayley, the grandson of Henry Osburne Seward. He continued to own the property until his death in 1920. His address was given as the Carlisle Hotel, Kingstown, Co. Dublin. He left his estate and effects to his sister, Henrietta Seward Riddall, the wife of the Reverend Edward Parkinson Riddall of 4 Parkmount, Lisburn, Co. Antrim.

"subject to the condition that my brother Henry Osburne Bayley is properly provided for during his life."

His will was made in 1902 and remained unchanged at the time of his death. His brother Henry had been ill for many years with a mental disease and was in doctor's care in an asylum in Dublin. Life in Ireland has changed dramatically by the end of the 19th century. The Land Acts had transferred land to the tenant farmers. The Church of Ireland was disestablished and the Catholic majority had a representative number of MP's at Westminister.

National School education was made compulsory in 1892. The number of National Schools had doubled between 1850-1900 with illiteracy decreasing from 47% in 1851 to 12% in 1911 for those over the age of 5 years. The number of those who could read and write rose from 33% to 84% from 1851-1911.

The survey map of Cork 1899-1900 (shown overleaf), shows Wellington Square situated in a somewhat rural setting on the Magazine Road, surrounded by open fields. We can see Wellington Square Avenue, leading from College Road to Magazine Road. Perhaps this was the private passage way that Henry Osburne Seward did not wish to dispose of in his will fifty years previously.

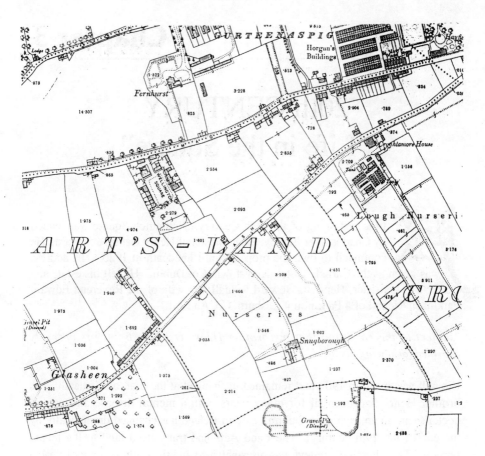

SURVEY MAP OF CORK 1900

Life in the square was also changing. From the wealthy upper middleclass, mainly Protestant occupiers, of the middle 19th century the census of 1901 shows the changes not only in the square itself, but also at a national level. It shows in detail the number of inhabitants in each house, their age, their standard of education, their occupations and religion. The census forms were filled in by the head of the family or in the case of the head of household being illiterate by the R.I.C. Constable. Our constable in this case who was collecting and verifying information was Patrick Sullivan. It is difficult to know which family lived in which house as sometimes the constables would zig-zag from one side of a street to another.

The heads of households in the square, their age their occupations and religion are listed as follows:

Name	Age	Occupation	Religion
John Peyton Glass	37	Shopkeeper/Draper	Christian
Charles Porter	61	Brewer	Brethren
Jeremiah Kelleher	48	Draper	Roman Catholic
Eugene Callanan	39	Accountant Cork Co.Co.	Roman Catholic
Timothy Cronin	35	Merchant Tailor	Roman Catholic
Robert Murray	68	Retired Army Vet. Surgeon	Roman Catholic
Jeremiah Crowley	60	Labourer	Roman Catholic
John Lynch	54	Carpenter	Roman Catholic
George Davis	45	Accountant	Roman Catholic
Margaret Forsyth	52	Widow	Church of Ireland
Alice Robinson	56	Widow	Church of Ireland
James Brushe	38	Commercial Clerk in confectionery business	Church of Ireland

With the possible exception of the Crowley and Lynch families the majority of the inhabitants would seem to have followed middleclass professions, such as shopkeepers, a brewer, and accountants. Though the terms " labourer" and "carpenter" might suggest working class connotations, we should remember that there was a Labour "aristocracy" of highly skilled tradesmen who perhaps had employees. The occupational breakdown in the square would appear to reinforce the strong social position of the rising Roman Catholic middle classes. These shopkeepers did not live above their premises as they had in the previous century, but had chosen to live in the suburbs. A move however which meant isolation for their wives who had previously helped in the running of the family business.

With seven out of the twelve households being Roman Catholic we can see the decline of the Ascendency position in Irish life. Out of sixty-five people in the square, forty-four were R.C, ten were Church of Ireland, nine were Christian, and two were Brethern. *(See Appendix for copies of Census Forms 1901).*

Another interesting fact from the census shows that only ten out of the sixty-five inhabitants could speak Irish. With the English language being the language of commercial and business interests, the decline of the Irish language is very apparent. The national figures which show the drop in illiteracy from 47% in 1851 to 12% in 1911, would appear to agree with figures for Wellington Square. Of the forty nine people of the age to read and write only four cannot, two being female servants and the Crowley household with two people over the age of sixty.

The position of women in the square is also highlighted in the census returns. Of the seven married women, none had occupations outside work in the home. Mrs. Mary B. Davis is the only lady to describe herself as a "housewife". There are ten unmarried women of the age to work. Eight are in employment, six being servants and two working outside the domestic sphere. Mary Kelleher, aged nineteen is a clerk and Frances Forsyth, aged twenty-two is a stenographer. Two of the houses kept boarders, the Cronins and the Glasses. All the servants in the square were Roman Catholic.

The information supplied by the census returns regarding the square would appear to mirror the changes at a national level. The decline of the Ascendency, the growth of Catholic middleclasses, the decline of the Irish language, and the position of womens employment. We can see the definite changes in Irish Society through the inhabitants of Wellington Square. The Folklore of the square, from the early 20th century remembers maids in the tunnels under the green, presumably fetching stores of a household nature contrasting with the stores of a different kind kept during the time of the magazine. Visitors to the square being asked to show their credentials at the gate lodge,before being driven onto the cobblestoned driveway in their carriages. There is a distinct "upstairs, downstairs" atmosphere in the square as six of the households had servants.

1930's

Henrietta Seward Riddall, the granddaughter of Henry Osburne Seward was in the possession of the lease of Wellington Square until her death in February 1935. In the event of her dying without children, her brother Charles had wished her to leave the square to and amongst such of his Irish relatives as she should see fit. In reading through the family papers of the Osburne Sewards, it is quite apparent that they thought of themselves as totally Irish though very Protestant. Henrietta left her property assets to her cousins, the Gregg family living at Tenby Cottage, Blackrock, in equal shares as tenants in common. The lease of Wellington Square stayed in the Gregg family until Nina de la Cour Gregg died on the 24th January,

1975. She died at St. Lukes' Home in Cork, formerly the Home for Protestant Incurables, Military Hill, Cork. What was left of the lands and property interests of the Osburne Sewards was left in trust to The Incorporated Home for Protestant Incurables, Cork, the Victoria Hospital, Cork, and Saint Finbarr's Cathedral, Cork for the upkeep of the said Cathedral Parish church. In her will the following legacies were also bequeathed.

Incorporated Home for Protestant Incurables Cork	£500
St Finbarr's Cathedral	£500
Victoria Hospital .	£250
Cork Protestant Orphan Society	£200
Buckingham House Free School	£100
Indigent Roomkeepers Association	£200
Society for the Prevention of Cruelty to Children, Cork	£100
Royal United Kingdom Beneficent Association	£200
Cork Cloyne and Ross Diocesan Board of Education	£50

The above list suggests the Victorian ethos of charitable work. As Matilda Osburne Seward had left legacies to Missionary and Protestant Societies in 1867, so too had Nina de la Cour Gregg one hundred and eight years later. It was in the 1970's that the residents of Wellington Square began to buy out the leasehold interests in their properties, with the Cork Community Housing Co-op buying three properties in the 1980's.

1950's

Through interviews with residents of the square, who spent their childhood there in the 1950's, we have discovered a colourful history from this period. A square full of children, a meeting place of football and weightlifting clubs with a social mix of people in a somewhat rural setting.

The houses in the 1950's were still rented with a fixed rent of six shillings for the smaller houses and eight shillings for the larger. There was a rural aspect to the square, with orchards and fruit and vegetable gardens. There were iron railings around the green, with six tall elm trees situated at the top of the square. These, unfortunately, were taken down later in the 1950's. A coach house can be remembered at the rear of No. 11 with the backyard being cobblestoned. There was a dairy and stables on the site of the Engineering works in the 1920's and residents can remember using the old horse shoes as shoe scrapers. There was a tunnel in No. 5, behind a timber door, leading under the green to No. 11. The residents of No. 5 can remember flooding in their kitchen perhaps as a result of the springwell. The advertisement in 1832 had mentioned *"There is an abundance of the finest spring water on the premises."*

Looking through the eyes of the children who resided in the square the memories of their childhood are very rich. It was a social, focal meeting point at the green area. The children attended Glasheen Primary School but it seems the whole neighbourhood of children met socially at the square. There was a weightlifting club in the basement of No. 11, our storekeeper's house from 1776. It was called the "Kasbah" and up to twenty people would meet there. With weights and pulleys attached to the ceiling, the house withstood more punishment at this time than in it's two hundred years of history. The Crofton Football Club also met at the square. Swings and ropes, twenty feet high were attached to the six tall elm trees which created something of an adventure playground. The place at the pillars was for talking and the games played were, "running bar the door" and "kick the can." The children knew well the folklore of the Duke of Wellington, of the carriages and cobblestones, and of the magazine supposedly situated at the top of the garden area 200 years before. With the large number of families in the square it was an ideal place for imagination and play. The Registry of Electors of 1951 names the residents as follows:

No.1   O'Mahony Bartholemew and Mary

No.2   O'Neill Eugene, Eileen, Sheila

No.3   Magrath Marie, Charlotte, Alexander

No.4   Leahy Samuel. Lambe Kate

No.5   McSweeney Catherine, Daniel, Cross William
        Condon Maurice, Nellie. Ward James, Bridget.
        McNamara John, Joseph Daly Jeremiah

No.6   Rohan John, Agnes

No.7   O'Connell William, Bridget. Cronin Nora Lynch Cornelius

No.8   Spillane David, Margaret, John, David (Jnr.)

No.9   Barry David, Nellie, Michael

No.10   Mitchell Josephine, Patrick, Anthony

No.11   Leahy Arthur, Kathleen, Leggett Andrew, Catherine, Eileen,
        Andrew, Maurice.

No. 12 Hennessy Thomas, Evelyn.

No.13   Staunton Jeremiah, Mary, Carmel.

The social standing of the square in 1951 was mixed. The occupations included a garda, teachers, nurses, bus drivers, and insurance clerks. The houses were still rented at this period and tended to be occupied by relations of previous residents when they left. Due to the age of the houses they were somewhat run down at this stage but the 1950's in Wellington Square still evokes an atmosphere of faded grandeur.

Mrs. McSweeney of No.5, an enterprising widow, kept lodgers and an array of guinea hens, turkeys, chickens and pullets at the side of her house. The guinea hen eggs were sold for 21 shillings per dozen and the feathers of the hens were much in demand. Their dark plummage mottled with white was used for decorative purposes on ladies hats. With farmyard stock escaping onto the green one wonders what the residents of the 1850's would have said.

ADVERT FROM THE CORK EXAMINER, OCTOBER 1953

The childhood memories recall, Charlie Gladstone who had lived in No.8 and his bells, and Cock Casey of No.6 the undisputed "boss" of the square. The Rohans setting off on their tandem for a spin on the fine summer evenings and the music from the Leggett's piano in No.11. It is hard to place Wellington Square in either a rural or an urban setting in the 1950's. It had the best of both worlds. The photographs donated by the older residents, dating from the 1920's to the 1950's of their childhood days, are a fond remembrance of their happy memories of the square. Many thanks to those who donated them.

The passage of time has seen Wellington Square inhabited by many diferent people, of diverse social class, religion, politics and occupation. From the early days of the magazine when James Lill acquired the land, to the recruits who passed through the doors of the Fort on their way to the Napoleonic wars. To Henry Osburne Seward creating an upper middleclass residential square to the Misses Seward epitomising the ethos of Victorian Life. To the Catholic middleclasses at the turn of the century who had begun to replace the Anglo Protestant life in the square, to Mary Mulcahy the cook in 1901 in No.11, and to the vivid recollections of childhood in the 1950's.

Wellington Square has been described as a 'gem'. It mirrors the changes in Irish society at a local level, and gives us a glimpse of the many facets of Irish history from the 1770's to the 1950's.

APPENDIX

Notes on the architecture of Wellington Square.

No.11, the oldest house in the square is a fine example of a Georgian building. Originally built in 1776 as the storekeepers house, many of it's fine external architectural features remain today.The Georgian period spans the 18th and early 19th centuries, and as only 6% of the houses in Cork City were built before 1860 the preservation of the square is of immense importance to the heritage of the city.

The house has many details typical of the Georgian era. Finished with cut Cork limestone and Dutch red brick window surrounds it has two stories over the basement and five bays.The windows on the ground floor are a variation on the Georgian theme as they have arched frames. There was an emphasis on vertical lines in architecture of this period with the sash windows being of greater length than width, with the windows of No.11 being finished with red brick as dressing.

Doorways were focal points in Georgian houses and No.11 is no exception. The original doorway has been obscured by the addition of a pedimented porch probably dating to 1832 when the other houses in the square were built. It contains a fanlight window with block and start dressing around the doorway.

The roof is of graduated slating and before the house was renovated there was weather slating on the small portion of wall on the gable ends. This was a typical external finish in the 18th century being a method to protect a wall by nailing slates to it in overlapping courses. Due to the difficulty of upkeep the weather slating has been removed, but the cutstone exterior has been retained in accordance with the desire to maintain the original Georgian character.

Though No.11 is not an elaborate building in Georgian terms, we should remember it's original purpose as a dwelling place inside a military compound. Though modest in appearance it contains fine architectural details in accordance with Georgian design.

The five houses on the other side of the square were built in 1832 in the reign of William 1V. They have the fine features of sash windows and interesting fanlights over the doorways. On entering the square part of the old fort walls are still visible. These two houses, No's 13 and 3, are built onto a much older wall which tapers outwards to the ground. No.11 was also built onto such a wall which is now hidden by the extension.

The garden walls although probably not as old as the fort, are built along the shape of the orginal outer wall of the fort - no doubt incorporating parts of the earlier structure and possibly using the same stones. They are fine examples of early 19th century garden walls having stood intact despite years of weathering and no apparent maintenance.

1. Number 11 Wellington Square

2. The tapering wall of the fort on number 3

3. The tapering effect on number 13

4. Example of arched Georgian window in number 11.

5. The entrance to the square

The Census Forms of Wellington Square 1901

CENSUS OF IRELAND, 1901.

(Two Examples of the mode of filling up this Table are given on the other side.)

FORM A.

No. on Form B. 7

RETURN of the MEMBERS of this FAMILY and their VISITORS, BOARDERS, SERVANTS, &c., who slept or abode in this House on the night of SUNDAY, the 31st of MARCH, 1901.

	NAME and SURNAME		RELATION to Head of Family	RELIGIOUS PROFESSION	EDUCATION	AGE		SEX	RANK, PROFESSION, OR OCCUPATION	MARRIAGE	WHERE BORN	IRISH LANGUAGE	If Deaf and Dumb, &c.
	Christian Name	Surname				Males	Females						
1	John Peyton	Glass	Head	Christian	Read + write	37		M	Shopkeeper Draper	Married	Shrewsbury		
2	Margaret	Glass	Wife	Do	Do Do		31	F		Do	City Cork		
3	Richard	Do	Son	Do	R Do	8		M	Prot Nand	Do Cork		
4	Ellison	Do	Daughter	Do	R Do	6		F	Sc.	Co Cork		
5	Martha	Do	Do	Do	Cannot read		4	F	Do	Do Do		
6	William	Do	Son	Do	Do Do	3		M	Do	Do Do		
7	Margaret	Do	Daughter	Do	Do Do	1		F	Sc.	Do Do		
8	Violet	Do	Do	Do			2 mths	F	Do	Do Do		
9	Alfred Richard	Kirk	Boarder	Do	Read + write	48		M	Accountant	Sc.	London		
10	Hannah Mary	O'Connor	Servant	Roman Catholic	Cannot read	34		F	Servant	Do	Cork		
11													
12													
13													
14													
15													

I hereby certify, as required by the Act 63 Vic., cap 6, s. 6 (1), that the foregoing Return is correct, according to the best of my knowledge and belief.

Peter J. Sullivan Sergt   John Peyton Glass (Signature of Enumerator.)

I believe the foregoing to be a true Return.
John Peyton Glass (Signature of Head of Family.)

CENSUS OF IRELAND, 1901.

(Two Examples of the mode of filling up this Table are given on the other side.)

FORM A.

No. on Form B. 13

RETURN of the MEMBERS of this FAMILY and their VISITORS, BOARDERS, SERVANTS, &c., who slept or abode in this House on the night of SUNDAY, the 31st of MARCH, 1901.

	NAME and SURNAME		RELATION to Head of Family	RELIGIOUS PROFESSION	EDUCATION	AGE		SEX	RANK, PROFESSION, OR OCCUPATION	MARRIAGE	WHERE BORN	IRISH LANGUAGE	If Deaf and Dumb, &c.
	Christian Name	Surname				Males	Females						
1	Robert	Murray	Head	R Catholic	Read + Write	68		M	Surgeon Army Retired	Widower	Cork City		
2	Vincent	Murray	Son	R Catholic	Read + Write	30		M	Journalist	Not married	County Kildare		
3	Josephine	Murray	Daughter	R Catholic	Read + Write	24		F		not married	England		
4	Benedict	Murray	Son	R Catholic	Read + Write	21		M	Artist (Painting)	not married	Co Kildare		
5	Norah	Scully	Servant Cook	R Catholic	Read + Write	36		F	Cook	not married	Cork County	Irish + English	
6	Patrick	Murray	Son	R Catholic	Read + Write	26		M		not married	England		
7													

CENSUS OF IRELAND, 1901.

(Two Examples of the mode of filling up this Table are given on the other side.)

FORM A.

No. on Form B. 11

RETURN of the MEMBERS of this FAMILY and their VISITORS, BOARDERS, SERVANTS, &c., who slept or abode in this House on the night of SUNDAY, the 31st of MARCH, 1901.

	NAME and SURNAME		RELATION to Head of Family	RELIGIOUS PROFESSION	EDUCATION	AGE		SEX	RANK, PROFESSION, OR OCCUPATION	MARRIAGE	WHERE BORN	IRISH LANGUAGE	If Deaf and Dumb, &c.
1	James W.A.	Brushe	Head of family	Church of Ireland	Read + write	38		M	Commercial Clerk	married	Co Mayo		
2	Margaret	Brushe	Wife	Do Do	Read + write	25		F		married	City Cork		
3	Wilfrid S.P.	Brushe	Son	Do Do	Cannot read	2		M		unmarried	Co Cork		
4													
5													

(Two Examples of the mode of filling up this Table are given on the other side.)

FORM A.

No. on Form B. 19

RETURN of the MEMBERS of this FAMILY and their VISITORS, BOARDERS, SERVANTS, &c., who slept or abode in this House on the night of SUNDAY, the 31st of MARCH, 1901.

	NAME and SURNAME	RELATION to Head of Family	RELIGIOUS PROFESSION	EDUCATION	AGE	SEX	RANK, PROFESSION, OR OCCUPATION	MARRIAGE	WHERE BORN	IRISH LANGUAGE	If Deaf and Dumb; Dumb only; Blind; Imbecile or Idiot; or Lunatic
1	Jeremiah Crowley	Head of Family	Roman Catholic	Cannot Read	60	M	Labourer	Married	Co. Cork	Irish & English	—
2	Kate Downey	Aunt	Roman Catholic	Cannot Read	70	M		Widow	Co. Cork	Irish & English	—

(Two Examples of the mode of filling up this Table are given on the other side.)

FORM A.

No. on Form B. 14

RETURN of the MEMBERS of this FAMILY and their VISITORS, BOARDERS, SERVANTS, &c., who slept or abode in this House on the night of SUNDAY, the 31st of MARCH, 1901.

	NAME and SURNAME	RELATION to Head of Family	RELIGIOUS PROFESSION	EDUCATION	AGE	SEX	RANK, PROFESSION, OR OCCUPATION	MARRIAGE	WHERE BORN	IRISH LANGUAGE	If Deaf and Dumb, &c.
1	Margaret Sheythe	Head of Family	Church of Ireland	Read & Write	52	F		Widow	Co. Cork		
2	Ena Ellen Sheythe	Daughter	Church of Ireland	Read & Write	22	F	Stenographer	Not Married	City of Cork		
3	Margaret Sheythe	Daughter	Church of Ireland	Read & Write	15	F	Scholar	Not Married	City of Cork		
4	Madoughan Sheythe	Son	Church of Ireland	Read & Write	11	M	Scholar	Not Married	City of Cork	O	
5	— McCarthy	Servant	Roman Catholic		30	F	General Servant	Not Married	City of Cork		

(Two Examples of the mode of filling up this Table are given on the other side.)

FORM A.

No. on Form B. 15

RETURN of the MEMBERS of this FAMILY and their VISITORS, BOARDERS, SERVANTS, &c., who slept or abode in this House on the night of SUNDAY, the 31st of MARCH, 1901.

	NAME and SURNAME	RELATION to Head of Family	RELIGIOUS PROFESSION	EDUCATION	AGE	SEX	RANK, PROFESSION, OR OCCUPATION	MARRIAGE	WHERE BORN	IRISH LANGUAGE	If Deaf and Dumb, &c.
1	Alice Robinson	Head of Family	Church of Ireland	Read & write	56	F		Widow	England	—	
2	Joseph McMahon	Son	Church of Ireland	Read & write	30	M	Architect	Not married	Dublin City	—	

(Two Examples of the mode of filling up this Table are given on the other side.)

FORM A.

No. on Form B. 20

RETURN of the MEMBERS of this FAMILY and their VISITORS, BOARDERS, SERVANTS, &c., who slept or abode in this House on the night of SUNDAY, the 31st of MARCH, 1901.

	NAME and SURNAME	RELATION to Head of Family	RELIGIOUS PROFESSION	EDUCATION	AGE	SEX	RANK, PROFESSION, OR OCCUPATION	MARRIAGE	WHERE BORN	IRISH LANGUAGE	If Deaf and Dumb, &c.
1	John Lynch	Head of Family	Roman Catholic	Read and write	57	M	Carpenter	Married	Co. Cork	Irish and English	

CENSUS OF IRELAND, 1901.

(Two Examples of the mode of filling up this Table are given on the other side.)

FORM A.

No. on Form B. 12

RETURN of the MEMBERS of this FAMILY and their VISITORS, BOARDERS, SERVANTS, &c., who slept or abode in this House on the night of SUNDAY, the 31st of MARCH, 1901.

NAME and SURNAME	RELATION to Head of Family	RELIGIOUS PROFESSION	EDUCATION	AGE	SEX	RANK, PROFESSION, OR OCCUPATION	MARRIAGE	WHERE BORN	IRISH LANGUAGE	If Deaf and Dumb; Dumb only; Blind; Imbecile or Idiot; or Lunatic.
1	Timothy Cronin	Head of Family	Roman Catholic	Read & Write	35	M	Merchant Tailor	Married	Co. Cork		
2	Julia Cronin	Wife	do	do	30	F		Married	Co. Cork		
3	Sarah Anne Cronin	Daughter	do	Cannot Read	4	F	Scholar	Not married	do		
4	Anna Maria Cronin	Daughter	do	Cannot Read	3	F	Scholar	Do	do		
5	Ellen Mary Cronin	Daughter	do	Cannot Read	9	F	Scholar	Do	do		
6	William Batersby	Boarder	do	Read & Write	20	M	Tailor	Not Married	Co. Dublin		
7	Julia Ahern	Servant	do	Read & Write	70	F	Servant	Widow	Co. Cork		

CENSUS OF IRELAND, 1901.

(Two Examples of the mode of filling up this Table are given on the other side.)

FORM A.

No. on Form B. 8

RETURN of the MEMBERS of this FAMILY and their VISITORS, BOARDERS, SERVANTS, &c., who slept or abode in this House on the night of SUNDAY, the 31st of MARCH, 1901.

NAME and SURNAME	RELATION to Head of Family	RELIGIOUS PROFESSION	EDUCATION	AGE	SEX	RANK, PROFESSION, OR OCCUPATION	MARRIAGE	WHERE BORN	IRISH LANGUAGE	If Deaf and Dumb; Dumb only; Blind; Imbecile or Idiot; or Lunatic.
1	Charles Porter	Head of Family	Brethren	Read & write	68	M	Brewer	Married	Dublin City		
2	Clara Mary do	Wife	do	do	66	F		do	England		
3	Ellen Mary do	Daughter	Church of Ireland	do	26	F		Not married	Cork City		

CENSUS OF IRELAND, 1901.

(Two Examples of the mode of filling up this Table are given on the other side.)

FORM A.

No. on Form B. 23

RETURN of the MEMBERS of this FAMILY and their VISITORS, BOARDERS, SERVANTS, &c., who slept or abode in this House on the night of SUNDAY, the 31st of MARCH, 1901.

NAME and SURNAME	RELATION to Head of Family	RELIGIOUS PROFESSION	EDUCATION	AGE	SEX	RANK, PROFESSION, OR OCCUPATION	MARRIAGE	WHERE BORN	IRISH LANGUAGE	If Deaf and Dumb, &c.
1	George Davis	Head of Family	Roman Catholic	Read & Write	45	M	Accountant	Married	Co. Wexford		
2	Mary B. Davis	Wife	do	do do	31	F	House Wife	do	City of Cork		
3	George F. Davis	Son	do	Cannot Read	3	M	Scholar	Single	do		
4	Mary B. Davis	Daughter	do	do	5	F	do	do	do		
5	Margaret F. Davis				1	F		do	do		

CENSUS OF IRELAND, 1901.

(Two Examples of the mode of filling up this Table are given on the other side.)

FORM A.

No. on Form B.

RETURN of the MEMBERS of this FAMILY and their VISITORS, BOARDERS, SERVANTS, &c., who slept or abode in this House on the night of SUNDAY, the 31st of MARCH, 1901.

NAME and SURNAME	RELATION to Head of Family	RELIGIOUS PROFESSION	EDUCATION	AGE	SEX	RANK, PROFESSION, OR OCCUPATION	MARRIAGE	WHERE BORN	IRISH LANGUAGE	If Deaf and Dumb, &c.
1	Jeremiah Kelleher	Head	Catholic	Read & Write	48	M	Draper	Married	City of Cork	English
2	Anne Kelleher	Wife	Catholic	Read & Write	40	F		Married	City of Cork	English
3	Mary Kelleher	Daughter	Catholic	Read & Write	19	F	Clerk	Not Married	City of Cork	English
4	Ernest Kelleher	Son	Catholic	Read & Write	17	M	Draper	Not Married	City of Cork	English
5	Frances Kelleher	Daughter	Catholic	Read & Write	14	F	Scholar	Not Married	City of Cork	English
6	Daniel Kelleher	Son	Catholic	Read & Write	9	M	Scholar	Not Married	County of Cork	English
7	Lily Kelleher	Daughter	Catholic	Read & Write	7	F	Scholar	Not Married	County of Cork	English
8	John Kelleher	Son	Catholic	Cannot Read	4	M	Scholar	Not Married	County of Cork	English
9	Jeremiah Kelleher	Son	Catholic	Cannot Read	3	M		Not Married	County of Cork	English
10	Mary Mahony	Servant	Catholic	Read & Write	37	F	Domestic Servant	Not Married	County of Cork	English

Bibliography

Deeds of Number 11 Wellington Square

List of Sales at Chichester House *1701 - 1702*

Hibernian Chronicle

Cork Corporation Books *1700 - 1800*

Board of Ordnance Minute Books *1773 - 1784 Royal Artillery Library*

Report of the Irish Board of Ordnance *1788 National Library, Dublin.*

Dear Old Ballina *Terry Reilly*

The Archaeology of Cork City and Harbour *Colin Rynne*

The Gunpowder Mill at Ballincollig *George O' Keefe*

Tithe Applotment Books, St. Finbarrs Parish

The Constitution

The Southern Reporter and Cork Commercial Courier

Seward and Bayley Papers *Boole Library, U.C.C., Cork.*

Griffiths Evaluation

Cork Examiner

Robert H. Laing's Cork Mercantile Directory *1863*

Henry & Coghlans Munster Directory *1867*

Guys Directory *1875*

1901 Census Returns

1951 Registry of Electors